KATE BLAKE

Lost And Found Purpose (by Kate Blake)

Living with a purpose

Contents

1.

2.

   1.

    2.

3.

   1.

2.

4.

1.

2.

5.

1.

2.

3.

4.

5.

6.

Preface

A life with a purpose is a life worth living. Living in a world that gives and takes whatever she pleases should be lived to the fullest. We have to live a life of fulfillment by impacting lives. Living with a selfish motive is totally living without a purpose.

We out to live a live that makes us celebrate our departure from this world not the kind of life that makes us feel like we were cut short when we get taken out of the world. Being able to live not just for yourself but for orders makes you live a life with purpose and keeps you going until your last days.

The the level of our success on earth is as a result of how impacting our existence was to others. Our life's worth is measured by how well we built others and how bad we destroyed them.

The memories you leave to the world when you leave can either be "Positive or Negative" and this would determine your how the world will remember, that's if they remember you at all.

* * *

One

LOST

Self conflict

Awakening in rush as she screams loudly like her head was about to explode, Kate was suddenly reminded by her 5 am alarm that she was only having a nightmare. Breathing heavily, she habitually stopped her alarm, sat up with her head facing down her bed while sweat ran down her face as she tries to gather her breath from the rambling.

After a 10 seconds of aimless struggle, she finally was able to capture and enslaved her breath to the control of her heart beat as she slowly repeats a tranquilizing breathing technique that got her totally calmed in 13 seconds. But, as she went about, from her bed to her writing desk the look from her dad gazing at her from a picture frame pierced through the heart of her mind, leaving the bleeding flashback of her recent terrifying nightmare, for the Ninth time, this same dream has got her up and shaking profusely like a fever stricken old man.

Her Black cat Katie seemed to be in shock as well, she slowly climbs her bed, rubbing herself on Kate's feet then jumped off as quick as a coward jumps off conflicts in order not to get involved.

She walked towards to grab her dads picture she felt her hands shaking, giving her a kind of restlessness syndrome. She had literally felt Anxiety kicking her, only that her spirit was far from her body which happened to be standing erect, holding a frame of picture like she was about to start wheeling at a funeral. Holding her dads picture, her doorbell rang!!

She kept still unable to hear the newly changed door bell as if a deaf garment swallowed her.
    She could only see herself walking out of darkness.

Running descending like a flash of light into her body.

Ouch!! She shouted as her blood spills from her deeply cut feet which seemed to be bleeding from her unconscious dropping of her Dads fragile picture frame which broke into her feet, cutting a little deep into her vein.

She quickly stepped away with her bleeding feet. Trying to get her car keys at the side of her coffee maker when she heard the bell ring!

This time it echoed in her head, she tried to gain control over herself but lost her stand, she slipped right in her blood, hit her head and blacked out into a wild hungry darkness.

As she floats in her dark world, she thought of her coffee maker, then she thought of her parent; she couldn't help but think about how loosing her parents might make a formerly "familiar world [appear] strange and unreachable."

She had just seen her parents involved in a car crash for the 9th time and the last dream felt like hands wrapped around her neck, it felt more real than life.

Then she traveled back in time to the previous day when she had heard her bell ring. Although after a few delay in the shower, the head to get the door.

Opening the door to a deliver box by the door step with a sticky note to it. With a smile on her face as she had just seen a familiar signature and a short sentence that reads "Happy birthday Our princesses, by the time you got this gift, we should be taking off from John F. Kennedy Airport from our 2 weeks vacation in New York, see you soon honey." She smiled heading back inside as she got a phone call. She picked up the call and said "Hello…………………"

"Beep…Beep… Beep…"

Kate opened her eyes to the ticking of the clock on the wall and the beeping of the electrocardiogram (EKG). She has been unconscious for 3 days now and no one has called for her, we called her home but an old lady who claimed to be the house keeper brought to our notice that she had just lost both parents in the New York City plane crash in a Queens neighborhood after takeoff on November 12, 2001, killing 263 people along side her parents. Her birthday was on the same day. What a sad news the other nurse replied as they both pack up.

They had just finished wrapping up Kate's head with bandages. She fell and hit her head so bad, they both continued. As they walked out, Kate fully regained consciousness. She thought of what she had just heard as she looked around progressively putting the puzzle together. Her eyes fell to the calendar on her table consequently drowning her in the curiosity of knowing what today's date is.

She called out helplessly like a dying child to the nurses as she tried to get up but fell down to the floor hitting her head by the electrocardiogram (EKG) she lost consciousness.

Lost

It is said that Betrayal annihilates trust. And that the more you depend on someone, the more deception is involved, and the more damage is done. But how can you not depend on the beautiful kind, loving parent that raised you?

The trust can't be negated because they formed part of your beliefs and ideas. They form up to 50% of your total memory. There's no way you wouldn't have absolute believe in the people that raised you, fed you and loved you.

Well! Like the saying goes; Each betrayal begins with believing in something or someone. When trust is broken, there is no medicine to recover that again as it was before.

They promised to always be there for me, I don't know what's happening but they aren't here.

Is it really true that One who feeds on promises eats from an empty bowl?

Because I can't tell what life would mean to me if they have abandoned me.

No!! They can't betray me….

They just made a mistake maybe in booking the wrong flight or something…

But, betraying someone once can be a mistake.

But Crossing someone twice is a choice and if I have been waiting for 3 days now,

As Kate was Lucid dreaming, listening to a voice as deep as the sea, she tries to comprehend the energy flowing into her soul, as she sleeps, so he reads.

Broken trust forces us to first acknowledge a painful reality but believe me, no one is ever betrayed, they only get what life has made available for them. Your situation would either teach you or enslave you.

We might become victims of our circumstances but we are humans, we are gods, we are hero's.

What we once enjoyed and deeply loved we can never lose, because whatever we deeply love becomes part of us.

I was raised by a single mother whom I lost when I was 12 years old. She had cancer and the doctor wasn't able to save her.

She's the exact reason I became a doctor, so I can help people who needs help so they don't end up loosing the people they love too early.

"You see, my father never taught me a thing. I never even saw me, I doubt if he has ever seen me.

"Only people who are capable of loving strongly can also suffer great sorrow, the people that have never had someone to love them would never hurt you if you love them

If I don't get to see you when you awaken, keep my voice in your heart. I'll stay there forever.

And keep this in mind, A great soul never dies. It brings us together again and again.

As Kate sleeps gently, listening to his voice, she totally drowns in his voice, as deep as the sea, she let's the energy flow, like the wave into her soul, as she sleeps, so he reads.

The tears that made the sea I cried,

    The struggles that carries the wind in it I lived,

    The multitude of stars that feels the sky, in them I was lost.

I was sleeping at the church, where I got chased out severally.

I figured I had to make it by all means since I had no one to support me.

I was only contorted by the stars at night when I lay on the streets, vulnerable and hungry but the stars let me.

Perhaps they are not stars in the sky, but rather openings where our loved ones shine down to let us know they are happy.

Grief is like the ocean, it comes in waves ebbing and flowing. I am sure to swim in it each time I thought of my late mother.

I lived a sorrowful life full of depression for so long. So long that I got tired of being a victim and at that moment, staring at a write up which I saw pasted on the wall which stated

"IF YOU DON'T LIKE YOUR STORY, GET YOUR OWN BOOK AND A PEN AND WRITE YOUR OWN STORY"

After that day, I told myself I will never be a victim ever again. I told up the decision of changing my life by writing in a book what I would like to do with my life and I am living your dream life at the moment.

As Kate sleeps gently, listening to a voice as deep as the sea, she couldn't help but cry silently, she was in grief as she sleeps, he reads.

Do you ever ask yourself questions that you probably can't confidently figure out the answers to like;

"WHY ARE WE HERE?"

"WHY DID I SURVIVE?"

"WHAT IS OUR PURPOSE?"

"ARE WE LIVING UP TO OUR FULL POTENTIALS?"

So the questions rang in my head days after days, nights after nights

I couldn't stop thinking about them until I was able to give myself a satisfying answer.

I came to the conclusion that we are here to make and impact, serve someone, care for someone other than ourselves.

Help people reach their full potentials.

And above all, live a life free of fear, depression, anxiety and worries because we won't be here forever.

MAKE EVERY SECOND COUNT!!!

You will lose someone you can't live without, and your heart will be badly broken, and the bad news is that you never completely get over the loss of your beloved. This is life, we can't undo it for it has been programmed this way by our maker. But this is also the good news. They live forever in your broken heart that doesn't seal back up.

They are never far from us, they will always live within us.

It's so much darker when a light goes out than it would have been if it had never shone. We are the lights to the world.

My mother is a never-ending song of solace, joy, and being in my heart. Although I occasionally forget the words, I always remember the tune.

Losing a mother leaves a hurt that will never fully mend, one that is unavoidable and inexpressible.

As Kate sleeps gently, listening to his voice, she totally drowns in his voice, as deep as the sea, she let's the energy flow, like the wave into her soul, as she sleeps, so as he reads.

Kate woke up to the same nightmare few minutes later, screaming and weeping trying to throw herself off the bed but the doctor was still in her room and quickly grabs her and held her still that she was unable to move.

She opened her eyes directly sat the doctor's face with her eye balls caught immediately by her doctors blue eyes.

She felt like she had just seen an angel, all she could say was "You are so beautiful" a voiceless word escorted by a slight lips movement.

hands round wrapped her. She struggled to fight but she was over powered by a calming voice, "stop it", she opened her eyes to her doctor, staring back at her, she was trapped in his blue eyes as blue as the sea, she couldn't even breathe like she fell so deep. She was trapped in the sea, she could only hear "beep".

Her nurse ran in asking Amado are you alright? I am fine, he replied, I think miss should be for diagnose for Parasomnias (sleeping disorder) he retorted as he walked out the room still staring at Kathryn with Kate staring right back.

Alright doc, the nurse replied.

Two

AND

On the fence

It may seem like everyone has their own preoccupations keeping them busy. In reality, people often just don't know what's going on in your head.

But if they did, chances are they'd be more than happy to lend a listening ear or help you find the support you need.

If talking to people you know feels too difficult, you can still talk to someone who cares and wants to

In a crisis, you might feel trapped because you don't see any way out. You might think you've blown your chance to have the life you wanted or permanently lost a friendship that really mattered to you.

Thoughts of suicide often stem from desperation and helplessness, but these feelings don't have to be permanent states of being.

When your emotions threaten to overwhelm you, get some distance by focusing on the facts instead.

Here are two important ones to start with:

Emotions aren't permanent. No matter how isolated, hopeless, angry, or lost you feel right now, you won't always feel that way. Emotions come and go, and you can learn how to better manage them.

Situations can change. Maybe you messed up or made the wrong choice. But continuing your life gives you the power to take back control over the circumstances and improve them.

You can make life more meaningful

Many people dealing with suicidal thoughts believe life lacks meaning or see themselves as a burden.

Giving up can feel easier when life seems pointless. But just as pain keeps you from seeing solutions, it can also pull the joy and significance from the things that used to matter.

Your life does have meaning, though. Challenge yourself to discover this meaning — or create it for yourself. It may not be large or earth-shattering, but it's still there. Consider skills, abilities, and other things you take pride in. Think about your connections with others or goals you once had.

Maybe you've always wanted to ride a horse, take a road trip, or visit the desert. Or perhaps there's a book or music album you've been waiting for, or even another season of your favorite show. No reason is too small.

Pets provide meaning, too. My cat was one of the main reasons I never fully gave up, and it wasn't just because he made my days a bit brighter. I worried about what would happen to him if I died, since it's not always easy to find good homes for senior cats with health issues and behavior quirks.

Mistakes don't have to define you

It's common to lash out when you're struggling, to do or say things you don't mean. The pain you cause can make you believe the people you hurt are better off without you, which can intensify suicidal thinking.

But consider this: They wouldn't feel hurt if they didn't care. Let this be proof that they care, and let it give you strength to apologize, make amends, or work on repairing the friendship.

Try opening up about the darkness you're feeling. Not everyone knows anger and irritability often show up as a symptom of depression or other mental health conditions.

Maybe you're feeling so miserable because you made a huge mistake you know you can't repair. You might see yourself as a terrible person. This remorse you feel, however, suggests the opposite: "Bad" people typically don't care when they hurt others.

Everyone messes up sometimes, and feeling bad about your mistakes shows you want to do better.

Giving yourself the chance to repair your mistakes allows you to prove you can, in fact, do better — even if you're just proving that to yourself. Your relationship with yourself is the first one you'll want to mend, after all.

Time does help lessen pain

You'll often hear suicide described as a permanent solution to temporary struggles.

I don't love this description, because not all problems are temporary. Time doesn't erase your experiences or change events. If you've lost a loved one or experienced trauma, you'll continue to carry that grief.

My lowest point came after a serious breakup. My ex no longer wanted to talk to me, though I was still completely in love with him. I was so distressed, I couldn't envision any future happiness for myself.

A lot of my feelings stemmed from my own dependency and the fact that the relationship itself wasn't terribly healthy. I've since moved on and developed other fulfilling, healthy relationships, but I still carry that reminder of pain and loss. The difference lies in how I've learned to manage those feelings.

Things really will improve, though you'll probably have to work at it. Your future may look a little different from what you envisioned, since not all damage can be repaired.

But even when you can't repair the damage, your experiences can still lead you to a rewarding future. The only catch? You have to give life a chance to surprise you.

The future isn't set in stone

Life takes courage. Period.

But the truth is, you just don't know what lies ahead. No one does. Things might get worse — but they could easily get better. Considering challenges you might face allows you to plan for them.

If your fear of the future tries to take over, consider this instead: Each day ahead is a possibility, a lump of clay you can mold. Your choices help shape the clay.

You can do things differently and maintain power over your fears, and a therapist can help you take the first steps.

You matter

And finally, hold on because you matter. However low you're feeling, remember this.

Life — and people — can always change, and you deserve another chance. Your life deserves another chance.

When you look back a few years down the line (because you will make it through this moment), you might find it hard to recall exactly how unhappy you were.

Your experience with the dark and ugly aspects of life will help you notice light and beauty more easily — and give you more capacity to enjoy them.

There's still hope, as long as you're still here. So, stay here. Keep learning. Keep growing. You've got this.

As she Kate read the last line, she looked at the door to her handsome blue eyes doctor smiling at her. Did you write this yourself? She gently asked staring at him. Yes I did, he replied.

Everything? She asked with amazement as she continued; you are so special, you could probably heal the world with this. How were you able to come up with such breathtaking words?

I was at a point where I needed help, I was at a point where I needed purpose, I found it in a sticker I saw on a wall, it stated

'IF YOU DON'T LIKE YOUR STORY, REWRITE IT."

Three

FOUND

Found love

Doctor took Kate out for dinner the next evening and they walked on the beach afterwards.

Holding hands,

It was a full moon and they stared at each other with the moon reflecting their heart directly from their eyes balls as it had a glimpse of the reflection of the moon.

Doctor said,

This is what I feel, could you tell me what it means after I am done explaining?

Yes, go On, Kate responded.

Doctor continued;

It feels like instant attraction with a bit of nervousness.

It's the feeling of butterflies in your stomach.

It's an intense feeling of joy, that can also feel a bit unsure because it feels so strong.

it feels calm, supportive and stable, a feeling of steady ease, confidence, and comfort.

I am concerned about the way I feel.

Why do you think I feel this way?

Kate; it's love because I feel exactly the same.

You're not concerned with the risk are you?

If anything, risk is what makes it exciting. Love pushes you to open yourself up completely to another person, to really be seen and understood.

And in spite of the possibility of heartbreak, we do it anyway. Love is a huge risk, but it seems to be the one we're all willing to take.

I feel calm and content around you.

It just feels right.

Love doesn't always have "good reasons," which is where the idea of unconditional love comes from.

There's a divine force telling me I'm on the right path. It doesn't always feel easy or even necessarily positive, but it always feels like I'm right where I need to be."

I feel like a complete individual.

I will accept the good with the bad.

Before getting to the wholehearted stage, couples have to go through disillusionment (the end of the honeymoon phase when faults start showing up) and ultimately, a decision about whether to stay together.

There's really no way around it.

Loving is realizing all the ways you're not perfect together and making it work anyway, and I am willing to love you forever

I trust you my love.

Despite the risk and any other difficulties, I want you in my life, and i promise I'll be around for the long haul.

I Found life in you

Life turned up in our own neighborhood: beneath the Martian surface, subsurface oceans of Jupiter's moon, Europa.

Or maybe the dream of the ages will come true, and we'll eavesdrop on the communications of extraterrestrial civilizations.

We might even capture evidence of "techno signatures," or traces of technology (think smog). Barring these strokes of luck, however, the job will be much harder.

Light will be the key – light from the atmospheres of exoplanets, split up into a rainbow spectrum that we can read like a bar code.

This method, called transit spectroscopy, would provide a menu of gases and chemicals in the skies of these worlds, including those linked to life.

But all I know is I found life in you.

Four

PURPOSE

Found Purpose

As Kate writes;

WHY YOU'RE SEEKING THE PURPOSE OF LIFE

Tony says, "If you're not growing, you're dying" – which is why growth is addictive to many of us. We naturally only feel fulfilled when we're improving ourselves or our lives in some way. Everything in life is calling to us to grow. When we stop growing, we start feeling pain, fear and anxiety.

As we turn around and observe what others have that we don't, we become vulnerable to jealousy. We begin craving prestige, financial possessions, and power instead of questioning, "What is my purpose

26

in life? But ultimately, all of those things will leave you feeling empty.

Setting goals, such as purchasing a home or starting a business, gives you a sense of accomplishment and is crucial to leading the life you want. These objectives are elevated even further by purpose. There is one word that will make you happy at Date With Destiny, I'll tell you that right now.

"Progress"

Progress equals happiness. Achieving goals does not equal happiness. So if you're asking yourself, "What is my purpose?," what you're really asking for is progress – a true sense of fulfillment. And fulfillment isn't a luxury or leisure activity – it's a necessity.

THE TWO THINGS THAT KEEP YOU FROM FINDING YOUR PURPOSE

You would imagine that there are numerous factors preventing people from discovering their actual calling. They don't want to upset the status quo since they are happy where they are. They are deluding themselves into believing they are happy because they have it all—money, family, and a house. Or perhaps they simply lack the time. The only two factors that actually keep you from responding to the query are, "What is my purpose?"

1. Certainty;

One of our most fundamental human needs is the need for stability and predictability. Routines allow us to conserve mental energy, and staying in our comfort zones can prevent us from experiencing anxiety and suffering emotional or physical harm. However, it also inhibits growth. It keeps us in bad relationships and unfulfilling careers. It keeps us from discovering our mission.

2. Limiting beliefs;

The narratives we tell ourselves about who we are have the power to either advance us or keep us back. Limiting attitudes such as "I'm not good enough" and "I don't deserve to be happy" result in self-destructive and fear-based behaviors. Finding our mission is made possible by our conviction that we are not constrained by anything in life. As Tony says, "We can change our lives. We can do, have, and be exactly what we wish." Believe that and purpose will follow."

BENEFITS OF KNOWING YOUR PURPOSE

Finding your purpose is associated with living longer, according to research. Nearly 7,000 senior citizens were polled about mortality and discovering your purpose in life. Participants who did not feel a strong sense of purpose in life were more than twice as likely to pass away before their time than those who did. The frequency of cardiovascular events like heart attacks and stroke was also decreased by having a feeling of purpose.

Even when income, race, gender, and level of education were taken into account, these outcomes persisted. Finding your purpose extends your life, according to research. Additionally, it is necessary for fulfillment and happiness.

Although knowing your purpose can help you achieve your objectives, achieving goals may not help you discover the meaning of life. You'll have a sense of clarity unlike any other when you properly understand your purpose because you'll be able to link the goals you have with your ultimate fulfillment. You'll experience enthusiasm, motivation, and laser-like focus. The best gift you can give yourself is to quit fighting with the past and the future and to begin living in the now.

HOW TO FIND PURPOSE IN LIFE

Knowing your mission has a lot of advantages, but how can you do that? The path to pleasure and a meaningful existence is created by combining the science of success and the art of fulfillment. You must learn to strike this equilibrium if you hope to find your mission.

1. SEARCH INWARD

The answers to the questions "What is my purpose in life?" and "How can I be happy?" are actually the same. By listening to other people's ideas and looking for outside acceptance, you can never truly comprehend how to establish your purpose.

You already possess all you require. Your own limiting thoughts are the only thing keeping you back. You gain more self-awareness with each limiting thought you recognize and replace with an empowering idea. You can govern your life when you have control over your emotions.

2. PUT PURPOSE BEFORE GOALS

You won't ever discover your actual passion or figure out how to find your purpose if all of your attention is on accomplishing short-term goals. You must always base your ambitions on discovering your mission. If they're not, you'll just get a momentary sense of satisfaction and will soon start looking for something else. The fact that life is happening for you rather than to you won't be apparent to you.

When you set a goal, consider how it will make you feel more content. How does this connect to my goal? To make sure that your mission is always in the forefront of your thoughts, use a journal or a system like Tony's Rapid Planning Method.

3. FOCUS ON WHAT YOU HAVE

Having an abundance mindset is similar to opening your eyes to life; you will notice goodness and beauty everywhere you look. Your life's purpose becomes much clearer with this new outlook. You feel like you have more answers and are closer to reaching important goals, so you start to wonder less and less about how to discover your purpose.

Fear leaves us and abundance shows up when we concentrate on what we already have. You'll stop worrying that your life is a waste and start attracting joy and optimism. Finding your meaning changes from being a difficult objective to an exhilarating journey.

4. TAKE OWNERSHIP OF YOUR LIFE

You can only find true fulfillment by creating your own life. You can achieve the remarkable by doing this. You must choose what is actually correct and be aware of it in your heart and soul if you want to discover your destiny. You must resist letting fear or worry control you. A choice chosen out of fear is never the right choice. It won't clarify the question "What is my purpose?" but will just make things more complicated.

You must give up playing the victim if you want to actually take ownership. Recognize that your decisions, not those of others, are the cause of every condition in your life. Fulfillment comes when you take ownership of discovering your mission rather than placing blame on others.

5. THINK ABOUT WHAT BRINGS YOU JOY

Consider your life's history and note the moments that brought you the most happiness. Was it at the time you two were interacting? delivering an effective presentation at work? Making art or giving back? You typically find your passions when you learn what makes you happy.

Examine your skills as well because they are related to that feeling of joy: Can you create a realistic portrait with a pencil? Do those who know you well say that you have a good ear? You'll probably discover passions that you may turn into a successful job when you pay close attention to the activities or abilities that come naturally to you and also make you happy.

6. DEVELOP YOUR OWN LIFE VISION STATEMENT

To answer the question "What is my purpose?" you must first understand the ideal world and your place in it. Finding out what life would be like if everyone was achieving their full potential is a necessary step in developing a life vision statement. This will assist you in creating a road map that will lead you in the right way.

7. DISCOVER YOUR TRUE NEEDS

Some people aren't even sure where to begin when they question themselves, "What is my mission in life?" If this describes you, it can be helpful to look at the Six Human Needs. Every choice you make is influenced by your primary desire, which may be contribution, love/connection, diversity, love/significance, or assurance.

Lack of self-awareness can cause you to have a false feeling of purpose that is actually based on other people's expectations. This explains why you can have the best physical health of your life, climb the career ladder to the top, meet the "ideal" mate, and still not be happy. Your innermost wants come first in seeking fulfillment.

8. WRITE OUT YOUR STORY

Writing aids in the organization of our ideas as well as the discovery of fresh ones. It has been demonstrated to aid in goal achievement, memory enhancement, and stress reduction—all of which are crucial while learning how to discover your purpose.

Writing about your life might uncover hidden meanings that you might not otherwise notice. Begin with this activity: What qualities do you possess that have enabled you to overcome challenges? How do you assist others? And how have others been able to assist you? When you put everything in writing, patterns will start to emerge that will aid in identifying your purpose.

9. TAKE TIME FOR YOURSELF

The solution to the profound question "What is my purpose?" requires thought and reflection. You never have time to just sit quietly and re-establish contact with yourself when you're constantly rushing from one engagement to another. Make sure to block off enough time for yourself so that you can tune out the outside world's demands and noise and concentrate on what you desire.

Take a deep breath and find your center if you're feeling worn out by your search for purpose in life. Spend some time on yourself, whether that means visiting a spa or relaxing with a book in the park. Your values—the convictions you hold most dear as a compass for your life—can be found by looking within. You won't comprehend where to look for your purpose.

10. EMBRACE ACCEPTANCE

Recognizing your limitations is a necessary step in discovering your mission. Give yourself a break rather than getting upset with yourself. Learn more about oneself gradually by acting as an observer. You can discover the significance you're looking for as you develop self-compassion and self-awareness.

Being tolerant of yourself entails practicing self-compassion. It can be incredibly unsettling to feel lost in life. Even though you might be frustrated, be kind to yourself. Every person who has ever asked themselves the question "What is my purpose?" started off in a state of ambiguity. Because of their hesitation, they dug deep and discovered deeper meaning.

11. FIND YOUR COMMUNITY

Finding where you fit in is frequently the first step in determining your life's purpose. We feel at home, at ease, and free to be who we truly are when we are around our "people." Your community can frequently assist you in learning how to locate your mission or, once you've found it, how to live it.

Follow your passions to find your community. Engage in voluntary work. Enroll in a class to learn a skill you like. Look for assistance online. Find people who share your taste in plays, literature, or music. You really are who your friends are, and when you find the perfect community, that can only be a wonderful thing.

12. BE FLEXIBLE

Letting rid of previous identities and activities that no longer serve us is one of the most difficult aspects of learning how to find your purpose. However, it still needs to be done. As you develop and change, your life's purpose is likely to do the same. You must be prepared to be adaptable and to pay attention to your innermost needs and desires.

Finding your mission requires a lifetime of effort. Being adaptable enables you to stay loyal to who you are while developing your integrity. What is my mission in life? will be lot simpler to answer if you define your basic beliefs and stop looking for outside validation.

As Kate writes, Amado(doctor) approaches her from the back, kissing her neck as he whispers "The kids are waiting in the car honey, we have to get going, this vacation is just for your birthday and we can't wait to celebrate you.

While whispering, Luis, Kate's toddler comes dragging mom's thumb "come on mum!! we gonna be late"

The all burst into laugh as they head for the car…

Five

Conclusion

YOUR LOSS IS A BIGGER GAIN FOR YOU

The world works as a result of applied principles. The world happens to reciprocate everything we give it. What you plant is what you rip.

If you plant the right kind of seed, you will receive exactly what you plant in ten folds.

On the other hand, if you plant the wrong kind of seed, you are sure to be reciprocated.

In every action, there's an equivalent reaction. Death for life, work for wealth, seed for harvest. It's as simple as that.

Everyone is sent in here for a purpose and a life fulfilled is a life lived with the accomplishment of its purpose .